JADA JONES
ROCK STAR

JADA JONES
★ ROCK STAR ★

Caring
Calcite ★

by Kelly Starling Lyons
illustrated by Vanessa Brantley Newton

Penguin Workshop
An Imprint of Penguin Random House

PENGUIN WORKSHOP
Penguin Young Readers Group
An Imprint of Penguin Random House LLC

Penguin supports copyright. Copyright fuels creativity, encourages
diverse voices, promotes free speech, and creates a vibrant culture.
Thank you for buying an authorized edition of this book and for complying
with copyright laws by not reproducing, scanning, or distributing any
part of it in any form without permission. You are supporting writers and
allowing Penguin to continue to publish books for every reader.

Text copyright © 2017 by Kelly Starling Lyons. Illustrations copyright
© 2017 by Vanessa Brantley Newton. All rights reserved. Published by
Penguin Workshop, an imprint of Penguin Random House LLC,
345 Hudson Street, New York, New York 10014. PENGUIN and PENGUIN
WORKSHOP are trademarks of Penguin Books Ltd, and the W colophon is a
trademark of Penguin Random House LLC. Manufactured in China.

Book design by Kayla Wasil.

Library of Congress Cataloging-in-Publication Data is available.

ISBN 9780448487519 (paperback)   10 9 8 7 6 5 4 3 2 1
ISBN 9780448487526 (library binding)   10 9 8 7 6 5 4 3 2 1

For my favorite rock stars: Jordan,
Josh, Ashley, Collin, Nina,
Katrina, and Gianna—KSL

For Coy and Dee with love—VBN

Chapter One:
BEST FRIEND BLUES

For the first time ever, I overslept. Usually I beat everyone downstairs on school mornings. But when I woke to the sun peeking through my blinds, I just shut my eyes again. I would have kept right on sleeping if Mom hadn't come into my room.

"Jada," she said. "It's time to get up."

I groaned and yanked the cover

over my head. Thinking about school
meant thinking about Mari. At
recess, we used to take off hunting
for rocks—inky black slivers,
orange hunks perfect for writing on
pavement, gray nuggets splashed
with silver that shimmered in the
light. Why did she have to move?

Mom sat next to me on my daybed

and gently pulled my fuzzy blanket back. My eyes blurred as I sniffed and tried not to cry.

I turned to the wall.

"I know you miss Mari," she said, pulling off my sleeping scarf and stroking my braids. "But you have lots of kids in your class who would love to be your friend. You'll see."

Mom kissed my head and left so I could get ready. I washed up and slid on my jeans with deep rock-stashing pockets and purple dragon T-shirt. I opened my jewelry box and picked up the heart-shaped pendant Mari gave me for my birthday. I clutched it in my hand. Her half said "best." My half said "friend." Even though Mari had just left Raleigh for Phoenix on Friday, I already felt like part of me was gone.

For breakfast, Daddy made his specialty—homemade banana pancakes with strawberry syrup.

"Can I get just a tiny smile from my favorite daughter?" he said, setting a flowered plate in front of me.

Daddy knew that would usually make me laugh. I'm his *only* daughter. I tried to smile, but it felt more like a grimace. All teeth with no joy. While my little brother, Jackson, gobbled his pancakes, I poked at mine with my fork. Finally, I washed down a mouthful with a gulp of milk.

Daddy put his hand on my shoulder.

"Blues can feel like they're here to stay," he said softly. I knew what he meant. Daddy plays all kinds of music—hip-hop, jazz, reggae. But his blues songs made me think of an aching way down deep. I wondered if the hurt of losing Mari would ever go away.

"But you know what's certain about the blues?" he asked.

I looked up at him and shook my head.

"They don't last forever."

I thought about what Daddy said on the way to school.

"Try to have a good day, honey," Mom said as she dropped Jackson and me off at Brookside Elementary.

I nodded before closing the car door behind me. Maybe it wouldn't be as bad as I thought. Maybe I could have an okay day without my best friend.

I walked Jackson to kindergarten and slowly climbed the stairs to the fourth-grade hallway. Miss Taylor had said we would be starting a new science unit. I couldn't help but get a little excited about that. But when I walked into my class, the first thing I saw was Mari's empty seat. I sat across from it and quickly hid my face behind my library book about different kinds of gems.

"Sorry Mari is gone," Lena whispered to me as she slid into her chair. She and Carson sat at my table.

We were the only group that now had three instead of four.

I put down my book and looked at her instead. Daddy said you could tell a lot by someone's eyes. Her kind, brown ones said *hope you're okay*.

"Thanks," I said.

Lena is cool. Her best friend is Simone. They are nuts about jump rope the way Mari and I are crazy for rocks. I thought about Mom saying I'd make new friends. Maybe I could show Lena and Simone how awesome rocks could be.

During lunch, I sat across from them and waited for my chance to talk. It seemed like it would never come. Simone kept glancing at me and frowning. She chattered to Lena about everything—what she did over the weekend, what movies she wanted to see, what she planned to do when she got home. It was like she was afraid to stop talking. Finally, she eyed me cautiously and bit into her pizza. I jumped right in.

"What can't walk but can skip?" I asked her and Lena.

"Huh?" Lena said, popping a grape into her mouth.

"It's a riddle," I said. "What can't walk but can skip?"

Lena shrugged. Simone looked annoyed.

"Give up?"

Lena nodded.

"A stone. It can't walk, but it can skip across a pond."

I waited for them to lose it. Lena grinned. Simone rolled her eyes.

"Lame," she mumbled. A couple of kids giggled.

I kept my eyes glued to my turkey sandwich. Mari would have loved that joke.

After lunch, we lined up for recess. I chewed my bottom lip and wished I could stay inside. As soon as I saw the playground, my missing-Mari ache was back.

"Hey, do you want to jump rope with us?" Lena asked.

I stank at jump rope, but the invite made me feel better. Lena and Simone were part of the Bunny Club, kids who could jump more than one hundred times in a row. They could do single rope and double Dutch. I loved their tricks, like hopping on one foot, touching the ground between jumps, and jumping so fast the thumping ropes sounded like drums.

"She probably just wants to look for rocks," Simone answered for me. "Right, Jada?"

"Yeah," I lied. "Thanks anyway, Lena."

I walked to the wooded edge by the swings where Mari and I discovered our best finds. One time, we snagged a piece that looked like pyrite. Covered with orange dirt, it didn't seem like much at first. But when I shined it on my pant leg, I saw sparkling golden flecks.

We didn't care if it was fool's gold. To us, it was treasure.

I picked up a smooth gray stone and a jagged brown rock and stuffed them in my pocket. Nothing extra special. It was no fun searching alone. I sat on the bench and watched my classmates jump, make up songs, and play kickball.

"Anything good?" Miles asked as he waited for his turn to kick. He liked rocks as much as he liked sports.

"Nope. Not this time."

"Keep looking," he said before running off to join the game. "You'll find something."

When we lined up to go back inside, I reached into my pocket and felt my smooth stone again. It wasn't what I was looking for, but it was pretty neat. Almost a perfect oval.

Cool to the touch and fit right into my
hand. Mari would give it a thumbs-up.
I bet Miles would, too. Maybe Daddy
was right. The blues weren't here
to stay.

Chapter Two:
TEAM TROUBLE

B ack in class, it was time to find out our new science unit.

"Before I tell you, let's see if anyone can guess," Miss Taylor said as her eyes gleamed.

She glanced my way and turned on the SMART Board.

A picture of limestone, slate, and quartz filled the screen. Lena grinned at me, and I smiled. We were starting

a unit on rocks and minerals!

As Miss Taylor filled us in, a spark of excitement flew from my head to my feet. I did a little dance right at my desk. We would spend one whole month studying something I loved. All of the fourth-grade classes would split into small teams. Each team would design fun projects to teach facts about rocks. Then there would be a rock fair, where students would vote for the best idea. The winner's class would get to go on a field trip to find rocks and gems.

"You can pick your partners, two or three to a group," Miss Taylor said. "But if you don't make good choices, I'll choose for you."

I looked at Lena and wondered if we could work together. She had invited me to jump rope. This could be my chance to find out if we could be friends. Just as I opened my mouth to ask her, Simone showed up at her side.

"Me and you," Simone said quickly to Lena, cutting her eyes at me and turning so I faced her back.

My heart sank. Simone clearly didn't want me on their team. Who would I team up with now? I glanced over at Carson's seat. He was paired with a friend at another table. I looked around the room for Miles. He already had partners, too.

"And Jada," I heard Lena say. My heart did a little flip.

"Jada?" Simone said like she couldn't believe Lena would suggest me as part of their group. I held my breath and pretended I didn't hear. Please ask. Please ask.

Lena tapped my shoulder.

"Jada, will you be on a team with Simone and me?"

Yes! I was looking forward to working with Lena. Simone, I wasn't so sure. Instead of Team Terrific, working with her could be Team Trouble. But rocks were my thing. How hard could it be?

"Sure," I said, and pushed my worry away with a smile. Two smiles in a day.

Chapter Three:
PROJECT ROCK

When Mom got off work at the library, I told her all about the rock project. She was almost more excited than I was.

"I'm so glad you had a good day," she said. "Let me know if you want to go on Saturday to get some new books about rocks." She was the children's librarian at Richard B. Harrison Library, one of my favorite

places. "Who's on your team?"

"You know Lena," I told her. "She was in my third-grade class and sits at my table. And Simone. Simone is part of Lena's jump-rope group. She's . . . all right."

Mom seemed to miss that last part.

"What did I tell you, Jada?" she chirped, and squeezed my hands. "Friends already. What are you thinking of doing?"

"I don't know," I said. "I want our project to be something creative and cool. Mari and I always came up with great ideas together."

I must have sounded pretty pitiful, because before I knew it, Jackson ran to his room and came down with the rock friend he made in class. It was painted green with crooked googly eyes. He held him out to me.

"You can borrow Charley," my brother offered. "Just promise to give him back."

"Thanks, Jax, but we have to make our own project."

He shrugged and patted Charley as he walked away. Sometimes Jackson got on my nerves. But right then, my little brother was okay.

The next time we had science, Miss Taylor put a trio of rocks on the table at the front of our classroom.

"Can anybody name the three types of rocks?"

My hand shot up. Miles's did, too.

"Jada."

"Sedimentary, igneous, and metamorphic."

"Know-it-all," I heard someone sneer under her breath. It sounded like Simone.

"You got it," Miss Taylor said. "Who knows what rocks are made of?"

Miles beat me that time.

"Minerals," he answered.

After we learned about the rock cycle, Miss Taylor gave us time to talk about our projects. Lena, Simone, and I found a meeting spot on the orange-and-blue-striped carpet.

"Let's come up with a list and choose the idea we like best," I suggested, turning to a fresh page in my lavender science journal.

"Who made you the boss?" Simone said.

"Well, how do you want to do it?"

"I already know what we should make," she said. "Rock stars. Everybody knows rocks are *bor-ing*. We can give ours eyelashes, fancy hair, and glam accessories." It sounded like Simone wanted to make a rock twin. Something always sparkled on her clothes. She showed her style from head to toe. "That's cool, right, Lena?"

Lena nodded. I couldn't believe it. Sure, they would be cute. But all I could think about was Charley, my little brother's rock buddy. Jackson was in kindergarten. We could do better than that. Plus, what does a rock star have to do with learning facts?

"It sounds nice," Lena said. "But I want to hear Jada's ideas, too."

All right!

"I have a bunch. We could make a gallery that compares the hardness of rocks, freeze different rocks and see what happens, write a rock rap . . ."

Simone yawned.

"*Bor*-ing. We want to win, right? Rock stars are the way to go."

"What does that have to do with learning about rocks?" There, I said it.

Simone rolled her eyes.

"Do I have to do everything? I already came up with the winning idea. You and Lena can work on the facts."

Mari would never insist on doing things her way. We always listened to each other and figured out what worked best for both of us.

"I think we should keep talking," I said. "What do you want to do, Lena?"

"Let's just vote," Simone insisted. "Who's for rock stars?"

Simone raised her hand. Lena looked from Simone to me and back again. I could tell she didn't know what to do.

"Come on, Lena," Simone urged.

This was terrible. I wished Mari was still here. I wished Simone was in another group. I wished I could just work by myself. I wished . . . I couldn't take it anymore.

"Fine! We can do rock stars!"

"Girls," Miss Taylor said sharply, looking right at me. "Is there a problem?"

"No, Miss Taylor," I said while Simone smirked.

I knew rock stars weren't even close to the best we could do, but I didn't care. My BFF lived across the country. Simone kept messing up my chance to be buddies with Lena, and now she was turning our science project into a disaster.

With Mari gone, nothing would ever be the same.

Chapter Four:
OPERATION KINDNESS

When I got home from school on Friday, I headed straight for my room. That was the day Daddy got off early from work. After school, we would build runs and ramps for marbles and make block forts and castles. Daddy was an engineer, so he always came up with cool designs.

"Jada, you have mail," Daddy

yelled from downstairs.

It was probably *National Geographic Kids*. But even getting one of my favorite magazines couldn't lift my gloomy mood. I dragged myself down the steps. When I got to the bottom, Daddy held out a postcard instead.

"Wonder who this is from?" he said innocently.

The front had a picture of the Grand Canyon. My heart skipped, and I held it to my chest. Mari!

"Thanks, Dad!"

I ran up to my room and flipped the postcard over and saw her pretty writing. She always loved my four-in-one pen, so I gave her one before she left. She could click and pick between colors, including turquoise, pink, and green. But Mari had used purple, the color we both liked best.

Jada! I wish you were here to see this with me. It's amazing. Ribbons of colored rock everywhere you look. The best part of being in Arizona: checking out all the awesome rocks. The worst part: being so far away from you. But guess what? Mom let me buy some stuff from the rock and gem store. I got a few things for you. I'll send them to you soon.

Rock on,

Mari

No matter what happened, Mari always found something to be happy about. Maybe that's what I needed to do, too. Even though Simone was a pain, Lena was definitely a keeper. If I tried harder with Simone, could we all be friends?

I read Mari's postcard again. She
was one of the sweetest people I
knew. I bet even Simone couldn't
be mean to her. On Monday I was
starting Operation Kindness.

At recess, I invited Simone and
Lena to go rock hunting with me.

"We can find rocks for our project,"
I said.

Simone couldn't argue with
that . . . I hoped.

"Great idea," Lena said.

"Okay," Simone said reluctantly.

I took them to some of the top
spots Mari and I explored: by the
swings, around the big shady tree

whose branches looked like leafy arms, in the gravel near the basketball hoop, on the hill that led to the fence. At first, we didn't discover anything exciting. Then I poked around and pulled out a rock that looked different from what I usually find. As I wiped

it off we could see it was special. Cloudy in spots and clear in others, it looked like quartz.

"That's so pretty," Lena said.

"Here, Simone, you can have it."
I held out my hand and offered it to
her.

She looked surprised. Then her
hazel eyes softened. Her caramel face
glowed. Her lips turned up, and what
do you know, she smiled.

"Thanks," she said, turning the crystal in her hand before tucking it into her jeans pocket. I thought my plan was working. But the longer we hunted, the more Simone stared at the jumpers and nudged Lena.

"Come on," she said to Lena, her tapping foot making her pink sneaker light up. "I'm ready to jump."

I tried to think fast.

"If we look hard, maybe we can find some glittery rocks, too."

Simone grabbed Lena's arm and started pulling.

"Let go," Lena said, and snatched her arm back. "You go ahead, Simone. I'll jump tomorrow."

"But you're the best turner," she

whined. "You're really going to miss jumping for some dumb rocks?"

"Just for one day."

I couldn't believe Lena was standing up to Simone and wanted to keep hunting. Simone rolled her eyes and stomped off.

Score one for me.

Chapter Five:
THE MAKING
OF A ROCK STAR

"What do you call someone who is boring and has rocks on the brain?" Simone asked Lena as we lined up after recess.

Lena frowned. Simone didn't wait for her to answer.

"A rock head," she said, staring at me.

"That's not cool, Simone," Miles said.

"Yeah," Lena said. "Back off."

My stomach twisted as I thought
about the surprise I had in my cubby
at school. Miss Taylor told me I
could bring in my rock-and-mineral

collection to show the class. Simone was really going to tease me after I took it out. Sharing didn't seem so fun anymore.

As soon as we got back to our classroom, I rushed over to Miss Taylor, trying to tell her I had changed my mind. She smiled at me and told everyone to settle down.

"Class, Jada has something special to show you."

Too late. I trudged over to my cubby, trying to not make eye contact with Simone. I pulled out my clear tackle box of rocks. They rumbled as I walked to the front of the class.

"This is graphite," I said, holding a shiny black chunk between my thumb and pointer finger. "It's used in pencils."

"This one is granite." I held out a nugget for everyone to see.

"This is my birthstone—amethyst.

"I got some of these as presents. But I found others around the playground with Mari."

Mari. Just saying her name made me feel like a jawbreaker was stuck in my throat. No matter how much I swallowed, it wouldn't go down. When I looked at her empty seat, my bottom lip started quivering. Then all of a sudden, my classmates started talking at once.

"Oh, can you pass them around, Jada?" Miles said.

"Yeah, Miss Taylor," Lena said. "Can Jada pass them around?"

"Please," the class sang like a chorus.

"Okay, okay," Miss Taylor said, laughing. "We can look at Jada's rocks, and then it's time to work on your projects."

"Yay!" they cheered.

I took a few of the best ones out of my box and gave one to each table.

"This amethyst looks like purple ice," Gabi said as she held it up to the light.

"Is that a geode?" Kyla asked, marveling at the crystal world inside a piece of dark gray rock.

"Cool! You have obsidian," Miles

said, checking out a black, glassy piece. "I don't even have that."

Simone sat on her hands and shook her head when it was her turn. She didn't want to see any of them.

After sharing, it was time to talk about next steps for our project.

"We found some good rocks," I said. "Now we need to figure out style. Simone, what do you think?"

Before she could answer, Gabi leaned over.

"Your rocks rock, Jada!" she said. "Do you think you can help me find some?"

"Sure."

"Just do whatever you want," Simone snapped.

"What's wrong, Simone?" Lena asked. Instead of answering, Simone crossed her arms.

For the rest of science, Lena and I swapped ideas while Simone pouted.

The next day at recess, when I started to search for rocks, Lena came over and started hunting with me. Then Gabi came, and then Miles. Then the singing crew and the rest of the kickball kids. Before I knew it, we had a rock-hunting party.

"Where did you find that quartz again?" Carson asked.

"I hope I find pyrite," Gabi said.

It was as if everyone was wild for rocks. Everyone, that is, except Simone.

With the jumpers searching for rocks, she sat on the bench alone. She didn't look angry anymore, just kind of sad.

At home, I raced upstairs, opened my desk drawer, grabbed my four-in-one pen, and clicked to purple.

Mari,

You'll never guess what happened at recess today! Almost our whole class started hunting for rocks. Everyone was asking me what to do and where to find the best ones. I felt like a real-life rock star. It was so cool. The only thing missing was you.

Rock on,

Jada

Chapter Six:
ALL THAT GLITTERS

When I got to school, kids were waiting for me.

"Jada, have you ever found an emerald?" Gabi wanted to know as I hung my backpack in my cubby.

"Once, the library where my mom works had a mobile gemstone guy come for after-school adventures," I said. "It wasn't shiny like you

see in pictures. But it was cool."

"How about a moonstone?" Carson asked, walking with me to our table.

"Nope. Not yet."

"Hey, Jada," Lena said when I sat down. "Can I hunt with you today?"

"Yeah!"

Talking to her felt good, like a hug from an old friend.

"You want to hear a joke?" I asked her. "What did the rock say to the hammer?"

"What?"

"You crack me up."

Lena's eyes crinkled, and her laughter rang across the room just like Mari's.

"Girls, I assume your morning work is finished," Miss Taylor said, looking at us from her desk.

I started writing in my journal.

Finding a rock is cool. Finding a friend is even better.

I sat between Gabi and Lena at lunch. Simone ate a couple of seats down from us and didn't say much. At recess, Simone jumped rope by herself while the rest of us searched for rocks. Every time I heard the rope hit the pavement, I wondered if I should ask her to join us. But I just kept on digging. Part of me felt like she deserved it. Part of me felt bad

for feeling like that. When we lined
up and she was right in front of me,
I decided to try again.

"Hi, Simone," I said.

She turned around and frowned

when she saw it was me. She faced forward without saying a word. I felt smaller than a pebble. I went from losing my best friend to having lots of new friends to wanting to be friends with the one person who didn't like me.

My mom always says, "All that glitters isn't gold." Now I know what she means.

Chapter Seven: WHAT REALLY ROCKS

Simone wasn't talking to me. And she was giving Lena the Popsicle treatment, too. She asked Miss Taylor if she could work with another team. After Miss Taylor walked our class to art on Thursday, she took the three of us into the hallway.

"I don't know what's going on with you," she said. "Who wants to tell me?"

We didn't say anything.

"All right, I can't make you share what's wrong," she said. "But you girls have a week to figure it out. That's when your *team* project is due."

A week to go. What were we going

to do? When I got home, I just wanted to flop into bed. But a small brown package sat on top of my blanket. As I walked closer, I saw my name written in neat purple letters. Mari! I tore it open and read her note.

Here are some rocks to add to your collection.

Rock on,
Mari

Light green and sharp like the point of a star. Peach and grainy like glitter mixed with sand. Blue with stripes like ocean waves. They were all so unique. I looked at the rocks and thought about Simone, Lena, and me. We were like that. Different but special in our own way. What if each of our rock stars had different personalities just like us? To tie in the facts, we could list their properties.

I asked Mom if I could invite Lena and Simone over to work on our project that weekend.

★

When I saw Simone in the hallway, I took a breath and walked her way.

"Want to come over to my house tomorrow?" I said.

"Why? Is your house made of rocks, too?"

That did it.

"Why do you have to be so nasty? What did I do to you?"

We stood face-to-face in the stairway landing, glaring at each other. Kids whispered and pointed at us as they walked by.

"Your best friend is gone, so you took mine," she snapped.

My mouth was open, but nothing came out. Is that what she thought? I remembered how terrible I felt when Mari left. Did Simone feel the same way?

"No, I didn't," I finally said softly. "I mean, I didn't mean to. I wanted to be your friend, too."

Simone twisted her lips like she didn't believe me. Then she stomped up the steps. But in class, I caught her glancing at me like she had something she didn't know how to say. When our eyes met, she looked away.

At lunch, Simone said hi to Lena and me. At recess, each time she jumped she moved a little closer to where we were rock hunting. I found a bumpy rock that shined if the sun struck it right.

"You should see this, Simone," I called.

"Yeah, Simone, check this out," Lena said.

She craned her neck and then dropped the rope and came over. She picked up the rock and frowned. Oh no. Not again.

She held it to her ear like an earring and struck a pose.

"Now that's how you rock a rock."

We laughed. I told Simone and Lena my idea for making rock stars with our personalities. They loved it. By the end of recess, it felt like we were on the way to being buddies.

On Saturday, Mom helped me set up a craft table in the family room. We put out glue, construction paper, different pieces of felt, and some rocks and minerals from

my collection. Then we made dirt
pudding cups with bits of rock candy
hidden in them. We put them in the
refrigerator and waited.

When I heard the doorbell, I
hit the music. If we were making
rock stars, we had to go all the way.
Simone arrived first. She added
sequins, glitter, sparkly pipe cleaners,
and a couple of rocks from the
playground to our supplies. Lena

brought buttons, yarn, and a few of her finds. We were ready to create.

The next week it was time for Brookside Rocks, the science fair to show our projects. There were crystals formed in a cup, floating rocks, and a mound of mock rock that kids could dig into to find fossils. Miles's team made one of the coolest projects—a board game called Rock and Roll. The playing pieces were rocks. You rolled dice to move around the board and learned facts about rocks and gems along the way.

Our rock-and-mineral stars were a hit, too. Glamorous Granite. That was

Glamorous
Granite

Caring
Calcite

Fearless
Feldspar

Simone. It had a yarn ponytail and leopard-print scarf. Lena was Caring Calcite with a curly 'fro, warm smile, and bow. I wished Mari could see mine. I had a hard time choosing. But I went with Fearless Feldspar. I decorated it with braids and a string necklace with a paper heart. Not half a heart like my pendant, a whole one. Even though Mari was gone, she was still part

of me. I knew I was part of her, too.

After the fair, all of the fourth-graders voted for their favorite project. We found out the results at an assembly.

"I'm so impressed by the outstanding work you've done," Miss Taylor said. "You're all winners. But the idea that earned the most votes was . . ."

As she stretched out that last word, it was so quiet that you could hear a feather fall. I crossed my fingers and looked at Lena and Simone. They crossed theirs, too. Did we win? Did we win?

"Rock and Roll!"

Miles! I was so happy for him. For us. Our class jumped up and down and whooped. We were going mining for gemstones! If I found a ruby, Mari's favorite, I already knew I was sending it to her.

"Congratulations, Miles!"

"Your rock stars were awesome," he said, holding up his hand for a high five. I grinned and slapped it with mine.

At recess, I watched Simone
and Lena head over to the jump
ropes. Gabi and her friends ran to
the swings to make up songs. Miles
and Kyla joined the kickball crew.
Things were back to normal. I started
walking to the edge of the field.

"Hey, where are you going?"
Simone asked.

"Huh?"

"We tried rock hunting," she said.
"Now you have to try something
new."

"Yeah, Jada," Lena said, smiling.
"We'll turn. You jump."

"Deal."

I was great at finding rocks. But with jumping, I had a lot of work to do. On my first couple of tries, I just made it over a few times before I stepped on the rope. I lost my balance and almost fell another time, but Simone and Lena cheered me on.

"Come on, Jada," Simone called.

"You can do it!" Lena said.

Ten. Eleven. Twelve. Thirteen. I was jumping without a miss! Each time I sailed over the rope, I felt a thrill kind of like finding a stone I never saw before. I never thought of jumping and rock hunting as having something in common. That made me think of something else.

"Hey, you want to play hopscotch?"

I asked when I was done.

"Hopscotch?" Simone and Lena said at the same time.

"Yeah, jumping and rocks, our two favorite things."

I used an orange rock to draw the lines and numbers on the pavement.

Simone, Lena, and I took turns tossing the rock and hopping. Before we knew it, other kids joined in.

I'm back to being the first one up on school mornings. Recess is different without Mari, but that's okay. I still miss her, but now I know that something else rocks—making new friends.

JADA'S RULES FOR BEING A ROCK STAR

1. Wear clothes that have deep pockets for stashing your rocks.

2. Don't judge a rock by how it looks when you find it. Sometimes you have to polish it or peek inside to see the treasure.

3. Invite friends to join you on your rock-hunting adventures. Then try their favorite activities, too.

4. Share what you know and what you find.

5. Dare to shine by being you.

ACKNOWLEDGMENTS

Special thank-you to the amazing Penguin Workshop team, my agent Caryn Wiseman, illustrator Vanessa Brantley Newton, all of my family and friends who helped me on this journey, and the following experts: Kevin G. Stewart, Associate Professor, Department of Geological Sciences, University of North Carolina at Chapel Hill; Dr. Chris Tacker, Research Curator in Geology, North Carolina Museum of Natural Sciences; and Walt Milowic of the Tar Heel Gem & Mineral Club.